DUE

DISCARD

The Disappearing Magician

Kids Can Read ® Kids Can Read is a registered trademark of Kids Can Press Ltd.

Text © 2001 Louise Dickson
Illustrations © 2001 Pat Cupples
Revised edition © 2007

Kids Can Press acknowledges the financial support of the Government of Ontario, through the Ontario Media Development Corporation's Ontario Book Initiative; the Ontario Arts Council; the Canada Council for the Arts; and the Government of Canada, through the BPIDP, for our publishing activity.

Published in Canada by	Published in the U.S. by
Kids Can Press Ltd.	Kids Can Press Ltd.
29 Birch Avenue	2250 Military Road
Toronto, ON M4V 1E2	Tonawanda, NY 14150

www.kidscanpress.com

Adapted by Louise Dickson from the book *The Vanishing Cat*.
Edited by David MacDonald
Designed by Kathleen Collett

Printed and bound in Singapore

The hardcover edition of this book is smyth sewn casebound.
The paperback edition of this book is limp sewn with a drawn-on cover.

CM 07 0 9 8 7 6 5 4 3 2 1
CM PA 07 0 9 8 7 6 5 4 3 2 1

Library and Archives Canada Cataloguing in Publication

Dickson, Louise, 1959–
    The disappearing magician / Louise Dickson ; Pat Cupples, illustrator.
(Kids Can read)
Previously published under title The vanishing cat.

ISBN-13: 978-1-55453-033-5 (bound) ISBN-13: 978-1-55453-034-2 (pbk.)
ISBN-10: 1-55453-033-4 (bound)   ISBN-10: 1-55453-034-2 (pbk.)

I. Cupples, Patricia II. Title. III. Series: Kids Can read (Toronto, Ont.)

GV1548.D525 2006   jC813'.54   C2006-902336-0

Kids Can Press is a *l***,©r**U**s**™ Entertainment company

The
Disappearing Magician

Written by **Louise Dickson**

Illustrated by **Pat Cupples**

Kids Can Press

Lu and Clancy are dog detectives.

They know how to sniff out trouble.

But even the best noses need

a rest sometimes.

Today, Lu only wanted

to sniff the salty air.

She was going on a boat trip.

And Clancy was coming, too!

Just then, a big dog

and a little dog ran over.

The big dog was Ruckus.

The little dog was Ruby.

They were Lu and Clancy's best friends.

"Let's go swimming," said Ruby.

"Let's eat," said Ruckus.

But Lu was staring at a poster

of a white cat.

The cat was a magician.

"Let's go to the magic show," Lu said.

"Let's go!" said Lu's friends.

A Magic Show!
Come and watch
Arabella do her
amazing magic tricks!

At the magic show,

Ruby helped with a trick.

Arabella, the magician,

was sawing through a box —

and Ruby was inside!

Swish-swish went the saw.

Lu and Clancy were scared.

The saw cut right through.

The box was in two!

But Ruby popped out safe and sound —

just like magic!

Everyone clapped.

Arabella took a bow.

The curtain came down.

The lights came on.

That night, Clancy dreamed

he was a magician.

He even pulled a rabbit out of a hat!

Suddenly, he woke up.

The ship was rocking.

"I am seasick," groaned Lu.

"Poor Lu," said Clancy.

"I will find something

to make you feel better."

He trotted down the hall.

Then a big wave hit the ship.

"Whoops!" yelped Clancy.

He fell through an open door.

He heard someone

talking on the phone.

It was Arabella!

Clancy was in Arabella's room!

She was talking about magic.

"I am going to do a disappearing act,"

she purred into the phone.

"It will be my best trick ever."

"Oh boy," thought Clancy.

"I can't wait. Her best trick ever!"

Next day, the water was calm.

Lu was feeling better.

And Ruby was doing

her own trick.

She licked a spoon

and put it on her nose.

It did not fall off!

"I wish I knew a magic trick,"

said Ruckus.

"Me too," said Lu.

"Maybe Arabella can teach us,"

said Clancy.

The four friends ran to Arabella's room

and peeked in the door.

They saw all kinds of things

Arabella used in her show —

magic wands, cards, coins

and rabbits in their cages.

"Wow!" said Ruckus.

Arabella was bent over an old trunk.

"Hello," called Lu.

Arabella quickly shut the lid.

"Can you teach me how to pull

a rabbit out of a hat?" asked Clancy.

"Can you teach me to pull

a coin from my ear?" asked Lu.

"How would you like to be in

my magic show?" Arabella asked.

That night at the magic show,

Arabella stepped out on the stage.

"Tonight Lu and Clancy will do

their mind-reading trick,"

said Arabella.

"For this, we need your finest jewels."

Arabella walked through the crowd.

She took a gold watch,

an emerald pin,

a diamond collar

and Miss Pug's pearls.

Arabella put the jewels on the table.

Lu blindfolded Clancy.

She asked Miss Pug to point to something.

Miss Pug pointed to her pearls.

Clancy took the blindfold off.

He put his paws on Lu's cheeks.

"Miss Pug has chosen ..."

said Lu slowly.

"Think, Clancy ... think.

What did Miss Pug want?" asked Lu.

"I think she wants ... her pearls,"

said Clancy.

BANG!

A door slammed.

The room went dark.

"Arabella?" called Lu.

"Arabella?" called Clancy.

"Where are you?"

Ruckus and Ruby ran over.

Lu looked at the table.

"The jewels are gone!" she yelped.

"And so is Arabella," barked Clancy.

"Ruckus and Ruby, find the captain!

Tell him we have been robbed."

Lu and Clancy sniffed around.

"This way," said Lu.

They sniffed down the hallway.

They sniffed all the way

to Arabella's room.

Her trunk was open.

Inside the trunk, Lu and Clancy saw

the gold watch, the emerald pin,

the diamond collar

and Miss Pug's pearls.

"Arabella is trying to steal the jewels,"

barked Clancy.

"I *am* stealing the jewels," she purred

from behind.

In a flash, Arabella tied up

Lu and Clancy with silk ties.

She dragged them to a dark closet.

Then she stuffed them inside.

Lu and Clancy tried to get free.

But it was no use.

The ship's horn tooted.

"Oh, no," cried Lu.

"The ship is going to dock."

"And Arabella is going to escape!"
yelped Clancy.

Suddenly, Ruckus opened the closet door.

Ruby bit through the silk ties

with her sharp teeth — just like magic!

"Ruckus and Ruby, we are so glad

to see you!" said Lu.

"Quick! Arabella is trying

to steal the jewels!" said Clancy.

The dogs ran up to the deck.

The trunk was on its way

down to the dock.

Clancy pushed the stop button.

The trunk flew

into the water.

Lu and Clancy dived in

and pulled the trunk to shore.

"And now for our final magic trick,"

said Clancy.

Lu opened the trunk.

Arabella was inside.

"Ta-da!" sang Lu.

"We stopped Arabella

from stealing the jewels!"

Lu and Clancy's Amazing Mind-Reading Trick

You and a partner can amaze your friends by doing Lu and Clancy's mind-reading trick (see pages 20–21).

1. Line up three objects on a table.

2. Blindfold your partner. Now ask a friend to point to one of the objects.

3. Remove your partner's blindfold.

4. Your partner should put her hands on your cheeks. Bite your top and bottom teeth together to let your partner know which object your friend has chosen. Bite your teeth together once if the object is on the left. Bite twice if the object is in the middle. Bite three times if the object is on the right.